Josephine and the House on the Hill

Enjoy the Stars!

Ron Broach

Published by Defender Publications, Harrison, TN, USA

First edition printed 2019
ISBN: 978-1-950038-08-4 (paperback)
ISBN: 978-1-950038-09-1 (eBook: ePUB)

PUBLISHERS NOTE:

Josephine and the House on the Hill

The Arrival

The house on the hill terrified Josephine. It was big and reminded her of a haunted mansion.

"That was twenty years ago," Josephine told herself. "Now I'm a college graduate with a psychology degree and a successful counseling practice. It's just a house."

As she walked up the path, the house seemed to loom over everything. The closer Josephine got, the more she could feel the pressure in her neck build. As she stepped onto the porch, she could hear her pulse throbbing in her ears. "This isn't reasonable," Jo muttered under her breath — but knowing it was unreasonable only made her fight or flight response stronger.

Jo pressed the doorbell button. Ding, Dong, Bing, Bong. The chime sounded like the carillon from the local cathedral. Jo waited. As she reached out to press the button again, the doorknob rattled and then turned. The door opened a crack — just far enough to see someone's eye looking out, evaluating the person on their porch. Then the door swung open wide, revealing an older woman with a grin from ear to ear.

"Josephine! I haven't seen you in years! Come in, how are you?" Aunt May continued talking as Josephine stepped through the doorway.

Aunt May.

Josephine's mind flooded with memories of fresh-baked chocolate chip cookies, huge home-cooked dinners, and family gatherings with all the relatives. Josephine felt her body relax. The urge to run dissipated. Jo's mind, however, refused to let go. Why did this house terrify her?

Aunt May continued her greeting barrage of questions and comments without needing to stop for air.

"Give me a hug, darlin', it's been so long since you've been here, step back and let me look at you, my goodness you've grown into a beautiful young lady, where are you working now? Did you bring any luggage, are you going to be able to stay all week? Is the rest of your family coming? When will they be here?"

Josephine tried to answer, but Aunt May never stopped. Jo wondered if she had mastered circular breathing. The questions about the family jolted Jo back to her current situation. Aunt May noticed the blank stare on Jo's face and stopped.

"I don't know anyone else's plans. We haven't talked about who is coming." Jo admitted quietly.

She didn't bother adding that she hadn't talked to her mom or dad about anything for several years. The family didn't like "psycho doctors" as they phrased it, so they gradually stopped talking. By the time Jo graduated from the university, they didn't even show up.

"Well, don't worry about that," Aunt May said in an almost comforting tone. "We'll find out if they are coming when they get here — or don't. Either way, it's not your place to speak for them. Let me show you to your room." With that, Aunt May spun suddenly in an almost military about-face and headed for the grand staircase.

Jo grabbed the handle of her carry-on bag and followed quickly as she wondered why Aunt May asked about the family if she thought it wasn't Jo's place to answer.

The staircase was majestic. It started in the middle of the room and went straight to the second floor. A balcony there allowed access to the rooms on the second floor, and space for a smaller staircase which led up to the third floor. Jo was disappointed when Aunt May continued up.

The Bedroom

The third floor seemed smaller than Jo remembered. The hall was narrow and went one direction from the stairs. As they walked down the hall, Jo noticed the doors were shorter than normal. Aunt May opened the door to a room at the end of the hall and stepped in, beckoning Jo to follow. Jo felt like she had to duck as she stepped into the room even though she was only 5'5" tall.

Everything in the room was sized for small people. The room was basically a rectangle, but the roof cut the ceiling at a slope. There was a window, Jo noticed thankfully, but it was in a cubbyhole formed by the dormer. The bed was on one wall, a dresser and nightstand on the other wall — neither within reach of the bed. "Oh well," Jo thought, "It should make waking up easier."

Aunt May turned to Josephine, "Dinner will be at 6:30 tonight. I'll leave you to settle in, please let me know if you need anything."

The room was barely big enough for both women to stand at the same time. Aunt May tried to slide past Jo, but her rotund figure wouldn't allow it. Jo put one knee on the bed and leaned sideward to make room for her aunt to pass.

After the door closed, Jo sat on the bed, put her head in her hands, and wondered aloud, "Why am I here? Why did I RSVP to a family reunion with people who don't like me?"

The Yard

After a minute, Jo stood and walked a few steps to look out the window. The dormer cubbyhole was barely wide enough to walk straight into, but she could do it. She looked out the window to see a beautiful view of the backyard. It stretched for several hundred feet to a wooden rail fence, and then on to a pond and open fields. She leaned slightly to look left. The window was dirty, so she reached up to wipe it off. With the dust somewhat clear, she could see to the edge of the backyard. The rail fence made a smooth curve to the side of the house, and then — there was a smaller fence setting off a special area. The family cemetery.

Michael.

Jo felt the hair on the back of her neck tingle. She felt a new wave of terror wash through the room. A thick, palpable emotion that was almost sickening. Jo staggered back and managed to fall onto the bed. Nothing could have prepared her for that memory. Even as she recited the advice she gave her own patients, the words sounded hollow. The struggle is real, find a happy memory and focus on it, deep breaths, slow thoughts. Calm. CALM. CALM!

Reset.

It isn't calming to scream the word "calm." Knowledge is not the same as implementation. Try again. Same process. More focus. Jo felt her heart rate slow, her breathing normalize, her tensed muscles relax. She realized her eyes were closed. As she tentatively opened her eyes, she saw the room was empty. Just the furniture, and her one unopened carry-on bag.

Jo opened her carry-on and pulled out a fresh T-shirt. She changed quickly and headed downstairs. Maybe there were more people, more distractions. Even if they were people who didn't like her, it was better than being alone with that memory.

Dinner

Josephine walked down the stairs to the first floor. The house seemed unusually quiet considering a family reunion dinner was only a few minutes away. As Jo reached the bottom of the staircase, she heard voices coming from the dining room. She turned toward the voices and took a deep breath.

It had been six years since she graduated from the university, and a little longer than that since she had spoken to her family. She stepped into the dining room and took a quick survey of who was there.

1. Aunt May,
2. Uncle Albert,
3. Jo's mom,
4. Jo's dad,
5. and now, Jo.

No big family gathering, no great sprawling dinner layout, just a close, intimate time with these few people.

"Great," Jo thought, "not exactly what I was hoping for."

What she said was, "Hi mom, hello dad."

Her dad was the first to reply, "Well, hello Josey. How's the psycho doctor today? Have you saved any lives?"

Her mom jumped in quickly, "Oh, daddy, you know psycho doctors don't save lives, they just sit in an office and let people talk.

It's like the perfect job if you can handle listening to everyone's problems."

Jo's mind flashed back to five minutes earlier in the bedroom. She wasn't about to admit that she had just worked herself out of a panic attack.

"I'm doing fine, dad. Thanks for asking."

Uncle Albert spoke up, "Well, now that we're all here, let's have some dinner. I had hoped more people would come, but it looks like it's just us. I'll say grace, and then we can dig in."

> Saying grace — it was something Jo couldn't remember anyone else doing in her life, but Uncle Albert had always done this before family meals; at least the big meals with all the family that Jo could remember. It didn't take long, it wasn't pretentious, just a few moments to "Thank God" for everyone's safe arrival and an expression of hope that the food would be good. Somehow Jo found that was discomforting. The safe arrival part was ok, but Uncle Albert had been eating Aunt May's cooking for what — maybe 30 years? Was he really still hoping the food would be good?

As Jo and her parents seated themselves on opposite sides of the table, Aunt May asked, "Al, could you help me bring the food out of the kitchen?"

"Of course, Maybel. 'Scuse us, folks, we'll be right back."

Aunt May and Uncle Albert disappeared through a door to the kitchen, and a deafening silence took over the dining room. It seemed the only thing louder than Jo's heartbeat was the ticking clock on the wall. Tick. Tock. Tick. Tock. Steady. Regular. Consistent. Sixty beats per minute. A normal tempo for a healthy adult. Jo could hear her heart beating at almost double-time, but not quite. The conflicting tempos adding another stressor.

"So, how's business?" Jo's dad broke the silence.

"It's good. I'm doing ok."

"So there's a lot of sick psycho's? That's quite a statement on our community," he goaded.

"Dad, they aren't sick. They just need some help getting through some particular problem. I help them with that journey."

"For a lucrative price per hour, no doubt. Great racket — you listen to them, they pay you. Gotta hand it to you kid, you found a gravy train," he kept pushing. "Not like us folks who work hard every day and earn a respectable paycheck doing something useful in life."

"I do more than listen to them, and you know it." Jo felt her anger rising, and with it, the risk of losing control. She remembered the kitchen had a door to the back yard.

"Of course you do, Josey," Jo's mom joined the conversation. "We know you went to school for several years to learn how to talk to these people."

Jo wanted to think her mom was acknowledging her education, but it felt more condescending. Especially with the pet name. Jo hated "Josey," and her parents knew it. It was a child's name — and she wasn't a child. It also rhymed with Mikey, it had been one of their inside jokes. They had both preferred their full names, Josephine and Michael, but couldn't get people to stop calling them by these other names.

"Mom, please call me Jo. I really prefer that."

"So now we can't even use the right name? How 'bout that mom, little girl gots herself an edumacation, and now she can tell us what to call her," her dad sneered.

Jo could see this wasn't going well and wasn't likely to get better.

"Excuse me," she said as she stood. As she walked into the kitchen, she could hear her dad's voice jabbing at her.

"You just gonna walk away? Why not stay and talk a while? Isn't that what you do? Hey, where you going…"

The Cemetery

His voice faded as the kitchen door closed. Aunt May and Uncle Albert looked at Jo questioningly as she entered. She ducked her head and walked faster. Straight through the kitchen and into the back yard.

When her feet hit the grass, she started running. It was dark now, the sun went down early this time of year. Down the back yard, running faster, the cold air was sharp in her lungs. She looked back to see — she wasn't sure what — and stumbled. As she slid across the grass, the house seemed to be watching. The window shades partway down like eyes, squinting through the darkness to see where she was going.

Jo rolled back to her feet and kept running down the hill. She collapsed on the fence, letting her body hang on the top rail, gasping for air, and hurting every time the cold inundated her lungs.

Jo hung on the fence rail for a few minutes until her breathing slowed and it didn't hurt. She stood up and stretched her back. It was sore from the fall down the hill.

She held onto the fence rail as she started to walk. The fence followed the bottom of the hill as it wound around the property. Jo realized she was walking toward the cemetery — and Michael. For the first time since she arrived at the house, Jo felt a sense of calm. The clinical side of Jo's mind laughed. How ironic that on a cold, dark night, after running away in fear, walking into a cemetery would be peaceful.

It felt good to laugh. Michael had always been able to bring out the best in Jo. They had met at a family dinner 23 years ago. Jo was 12, Michael was 19. He lived by himself a few houses down the street, and although he wasn't technically related to anyone, he felt like family. Aunt May and Uncle Albert had hired him to help with stuff around the house and then accepted him as part of their family. She remembered thinking that Michael was the most handsome man she had ever seen and smiled again. It was a first crush like only a 12-year-old girl could feel.

Jo was at the gate now. She looked up at the house. It had one eye open, watching what was happening. Not disapproving, just monitoring — or — encouraging?

Jo gently pushed the gate open and stepped into the cemetery. It was 100 feet across and 50 feet front to back. The gate was off-center to the right about 20 feet, and she was ok with that. Michael was resting on the right side, so it meant she didn't have to walk through as many people to get to him.

Jo knelt beside the headstone. The granite was smooth and cold. She ran her fingers across the lettering:

Michael (Mikey) Zaking
We didn't know you long enough.

Jo sat there for a minute, just remembering. Remembering the times when they would talk. Michael always had time to listen to her, to encourage her like the big brother she never had.

"Hi." Jo didn't expect an answer — and she didn't get one. Still, it felt good to talk out loud.

"I miss you, Michael." Silence.

She looked up at the house again. It was dark, no lights. Nothing.

"Hey, I finished school. Got my degree and license as a counselor…" Her voice trailed off as she realized he wouldn't have known about her interest in counseling. It was his death that pushed her into this field.

The memories of that day came flooding in.

Memories

The crisp November air filled Jo with energy. She loved fall, and Thanksgiving was one of her favorite holidays. She hadn't seen Michael since she turned 15 several months ago and was dying to tell him that she had been accepted into the Scholar's Club at school. Her dad was driving, her mom was in the front passenger seat. Jo had spread out in the back seat the whole trip, trying to look chill, but the excitement made it nearly impossible – especially when they passed the Volunteer Fire Station. That meant they were only a couple minutes away from their destination.

As soon as the car stopped, Josephine flung her door open and headed for the house. Her dad stepped out quickly and called her, "Hey, Josey! Come back and get your bags!"

By the time she got back to the car, her dad had popped the trunk open. Josephine grabbed her bags and headed toward the house again. Aunt May met her at the door with a huge, smothering hug that only aunts can give.

"Hello, Josephine! I hope you had a good trip. Are you doing well? I'm so glad you are here! You know where your room is, third floor, end of the hall. Settle in and then come back down. We'll have dinner ready real soon." It seemed like Aunt May could talk endlessly.

Jo headed up the stairs as quickly as she could, but her shoulder bag and suitcase refused to swing in rhythm with her steps. They fought with each other, throwing their weight from one side to the other — and never forward, the direction Jo was trying to move them.

Jo stopped on the balcony of the second floor to rearrange her bags. She heard noises down the hall. Michael stepped out of a room on one side of the hall with a paintbrush in his hand. He looked her direction, smiled, waved, and disappeared into a room on the other side of the hall.

Jo heard her parents come in and greet Aunt May. She knew she needed to get her stuff out of the way before they got to the second floor. Dad wouldn't be happy if he had to step around a mess she left on the floor. She gathered her bag and suitcase and headed up the stairs to the third floor.

She hurried down the hall and swung the door to her room open. As the door opened, Jo heard a crash. She tossed her bags on the bed and looked behind the door to see what had fallen. She didn't see anything that seemed out of place.

She faintly heard Uncle Albert call up from the first floor, "Hey, Mikey! Is everything ok up there?"

No answer.

Jo froze, waiting to hear Michael say something, anything. All she could hear was footsteps running up the stairs. She started walking down the hall, hesitantly at first, not knowing if she really wanted to know what happened. Knowing in her heart, it wasn't good. Each step got faster, she had to know. By the time she reached the stairs, she was running.

Jo took the stairs two steps at a time, reaching the second floor balcony in record time. She turned to look down the hall. Her mom and Uncle Albert were standing in a doorway. Jo ran down the hall and pushed past them into the room. She felt her mom and Uncle Albert try to catch her but managed to slip past their hands. Her momentum carried her half-way across the room.

When she turned around, her mind refused to acknowledge the scene her eyes were conveying. A ladder was turned sideward, lying on the floor. There was a can of blue paint spilled beside the ladder. A dresser was setting in the middle of the floor. Blue paint and red splattered on the side. Michael was on the floor in what seemed to be a most unnatural position with a red stain on the floor beside Michael's head. Her dad was kneeling beside Michael, his hands covered in red.

The terrifying realization hit Jo, Michael's fallen, been hurt, and her dad's hands are covered in his blood. Terror focused Jo's vision, the only thing she could see was her dad's red hands.

She yelled, "Get away from him! Don't hurt him!" and took a running leap at her dad. Jo managed to launch herself completely over Michael. She was airborne when she tackled her dad, knocking him on his back and then rolling off to the side. Uncle Albert tried to stop Jo, but she twisted and slid out of his grasp. She dove for Michael, wanting to talk to him, but her dad grabbed her. He wrapped both arms around her, holding her back, restraining her arms, the red stains on his hands smearing on her clothes — on her arms. Michael's blood on her.

Her dad pulled her into the hallway, still holding her tight. Jo was still struggling to get away, but her dad's hold was strong. She tired and slowed as the shock of what she had seen embedded itself in her mind. Her senses started to widen again.

She heard sirens pull up and stop. "Good," Jo thought, "Someone called for help."

As the medics came up the stairs, Jo's dad stepped into the room across the hall, pulling her with him to give the medics space to get by. They were bringing a gurney with medical bags on it down the hall.

She tried to follow the medics into the room, but her dad held her back again, "They're professionals, they know what they are doing. Stay back and give them room to work."

Jo's mom and Uncle Albert had stepped back into the doorway, blocking any view of what the medics were doing. She considered making another dash and breaking through the human barricade blocking the door, but that seemed unlikely to work twice. She saw the medics raise the gurney and turn toward the door. Her mom and Uncle Albert stepped into the room with Jo and her dad, making room for the medics to pass – still blocking the view of what was happening.

Jo could see the gurney leave the room and turn down the hall. They didn't seem to be in a hurry, maybe Michael was ok. Jo dared to hope until she looked at Uncle Albert's face. His expression said everything.

That was the last time Jo saw Michael. The family Thanksgiving dinner was called off, and everyone went home. Her mom and dad wouldn't — couldn't — didn't come back for the funeral. For days Jo begged them to, but they always had a reason: It was too far, there wasn't time, they couldn't get off work, Michael wasn't a family member... but to Jo, he was family. Then the funeral was over. Michael was buried, and Jo wasn't there. The resentment towards her mom and dad built a hard wall as Jo resolved to never let anyone suffer like she has.

The House

Jo realized she was leaning on Michael's headstone. The granite was cool against her flushed cheek, her fingers feeling the outline of the lettering. Her tears running down the face of the granite, leaving a trail in the dust. She took a deep breath and sat up. Still touching the granite, she whispered, "You were family to me, you would listen when no one else would. I felt safe with you."

Jo looked up the hill toward the house. There were lights on now. They seemed warm and inviting, calling her back to the safety and shelter of indoors. She stood and slowly walked toward the gate. Before she stepped through, she turned and looked toward Michael's grave one last time, "I loved you, Michael — I miss you."

Jo closed the gate and slowly walked up the hill toward the house. She realized she had no idea how long she had been outside. The light by the back door was on, so at least the house was giving her a guide. She stepped into the kitchen hesitantly, listening for sounds of the family. The house was quiet. As she walked across the kitchen, she noticed a plate of food sitting on the counter. It was covered with plastic wrap, there was a note and silverware beside it:

Josephine,
Left this out for you. Hope you enjoy it.
-Uncle Al

Jo smiled at the efficiency of the message. Uncle Al never said much, he probably couldn't if Aunt May was close, but somehow he always seemed to take care of whatever needed attention. Aunt May was always busy, constantly moving and chatting, while Uncle Al was in the background, quietly providing support for whatever was happening.

The clock on the wall said it was 11:30. Jo realized she was hungry, she opened the refrigerator and found a bottle of water. She picked up the plate of food, stuck the silverware in the back pocket of her jeans, and balanced the bottle on the edge of the plate. With everything in place, Jo left the kitchen and headed up the stairs. She hoped she could make it up to her room without running into anyone. She really didn't feel like talking right now.

She started up the stairs. It seemed like there were more stairs than before. Each movement brought the anticipation of a squeaky step, but the house was quiet. As Jo stepped onto the second floor balcony, she felt a sense of relief that the house was not betraying her. As she turned to go up the stairs to the third floor, she looked down the hallway of the second floor. The hall was dark, and the memories flashed through her mind again. Jo struggled to push them down and looked up to the third floor. She put a foot on the first step above the balcony. Her eyes drawn down the second floor hallway again, Jo forced her other foot up to the second step.

Balance the plate. Don't drop the water bottle. Focus on the steps. Move the other foot. It became a conscious effort to walk. Jo's eyes focused up the stairs again. Her muscles yearning for the end of the stairs.

Jo's eyes finally reached high enough to see the floor of the hallway come into view. At first, just a flat plane reaching out from the top step — take another step — then the floor taking shape as the flat side of an endless tunnel reaching into nothingness. She shook her head to try and make the hallway look normal, but it didn't change. Jo looked behind her, down the steps she had just climbed. The stairs looked normal. She looked down the hall — a long tunnel which decreased into nothingness in the distance.

Jo set her plate down at the top of the stairs. She turned and hesitantly stepped down toward the second floor again. It felt right. Jo felt the approval of the house. She wasn't sure why, but this was where she needed to go. Step by step, down to the second floor balcony, gaining confidence with each step until she turned and started down the second floor hallway.

Jo was two steps down the hallway before she realized where she was going. She tried to stop, but the house was pulling her now — a subtle draw, but firm — Jo stopped fighting it.

She found herself in front of a door. The plaque on the door read:

In Memory of Michael "Mikey" Zaking

Josephine put her hand on the doorknob, terrified of what she would find, but unable to stop. The door creaked ever so slightly as it moved for the first time in years.

The End of Everything

Jo stepped into the room, still holding the doorknob. Moonlight was coming in the window, just enough to see that the room was mostly empty. Still holding the doorknob, she reached behind her and felt along the wall until she found the light switch.

Click - light filled the room.

Jo blinked several times as her eyes adjusted to the change in light level. There was a dresser sitting in the middle of the floor. A ladder lying sideward near the wall behind the door. Blue paint was splattered on the floor and the dresser, smeared from where someone had tried to clean it, or — more correctly, Jo realized — where someone had cleaned Michael's blood. The room was a time capsule, saving a moment in history for her return.

Jo's mind processed the scene, and her terror gave way to curiosity. Why hadn't the room changed? Surely Aunt May and Uncle Albert would have wanted to finish what had been started. Jo let go of the doorknob and took a step farther into the room. Part of the room was the original burnt-orange color. It grated on Josephine's nerves by merely existing. Some colors just shouldn't happen. Then, starting in one corner was the most perfect color of sky-blue. It was spread evenly, smoothly, perfectly along the wall from the floor to the ceiling. It seemed to create a portal out of the house to a better place — a place where Michael might be. The sky-blue wrapped around the wall until it got to the ladder, then it stopped. Abruptly.

There was something wrong with the place where the colors came together. Jo walked across the room to get a better look. Her eyes couldn't focus on the color change. She bent down and grabbed the ladder, setting it upright she tested its stability. It seemed fine. She stepped on the first step, then the second step. She still couldn't see clearly. Up to the third step. Too high, her head was against the ceiling now. Why were ladders never the right height?

Jo leaned over to touch the place where the colors came together. The smooth sky-blue became rough like it was fighting to maintain its control over the burnt-orange. It was curious, after so many years, to see the paint fight for control. Instinctively, Jo leaned a little farther. The ladder shifted. Jo tensed. The ladder moved sideward, out from under Jo. She felt her feet move with the ladder, and her body began to drop. Her hands waved frantically, trying to grab anything, but all they could reach was air.

Jo felt her body falling, then bouncing as it hit the floor. Her arms, legs, body, and head all moving in a spontaneous synchronized dance, which ended in a most unnatural position on the floor. Her leg was bent the wrong way. Her arms were numb, she couldn't move them. Her head was wet with a warm, thick pool forming on the floor. Jo couldn't move. For the first time in years, she didn't care and let herself relax.

The blue walls filled Jo's vision. A peaceful, sky-blue wall of color beckoned to Jo. She felt herself being pulled into the blue at the same time she felt like she was sinking into the floor. Not like she was being pulled apart – more like she was expanding into new areas.

There was a noise in the background. Footsteps. Someone beside her, trying to get her attention. Dad. Jo felt him try to move her. What was he doing? Then he cried out and covered his face with his hands. Hands covered with red.

Josephine understood now. Dad hadn't been trying to hurt Michael. She tried to say that she understood, that she knew it was ok, but she couldn't move — couldn't talk. The sky-blue wall of color was everywhere now. Peacefully covering everything. Sounds faded. Motion faded. Just blue. Just peace.

Then nothing.

CPSIA information can be obtained
at www.ICGtesting.com
Printed in the USA
LVIC060509091119
636798LV00001B/3